Karen's New Teacher

Look for these
and other books about Karen
in the
Baby-sitters Little Sister series:

Little Sister

Karen's New Teacher
Ann M. Martin

Illustrations by Susan Tang

A
LITTLE APPLE
PAPERBACK

SCHOLASTIC INC.
New York Toronto London Auckland Sydney

For all those who have learned
to cope without

ISBN 0-590-44824-2

12 11 10 9 8 7 6 5 4   2 3 4 5 6/9

Printed in the U.S.A.   40

First Scholastic printing, September 1991

Arithmetic Pizza

"One pepperoni, two pepperonis, three pepperonis, four — "

"Natalie," I said, "you do not have to *count* each piece of pepperoni. Just spread them around half the pizza."

"Oh." Natalie kept on working.

You will never guess where we were. We were in *school*. Our teacher, Ms. Colman, who is gigundo nice, was helping us to learn about fractions.

"I want you," she had said to our class,

"to divide into groups of three or four. Each group is going to make a pizza."

"For real?" asked Hank Reubens. (Hank loves to eat.)

"Not at first," replied Ms. Colman. "At first you will make pretend pizzas out of construction paper. Later you will make real pizzas, just like the paper ones you design. Then we will have a class pizza party."

"Cool!" exclaimed Bobby Gianelli.

Ms. Colman is my most favorite teacher ever. I am glad I am in her second-grade class. Ms. Colman makes learning fun. How many teachers help you to learn about halves and quarters by letting you make pizzas? How many teachers wear a costume to your school Halloween festival? (Ms. Colman dressed up as a pencil.) Also, she lets us put on plays, she reads aloud to us, and she takes us on field trips.

Those are not the only good things about my teacher. She is also nice to kids. She almost never yells, and we can talk to her about anything — like divorce or a new baby or if we have a fight with our friends.

I know all about divorce. My parents got divorced. That was a few years ago when I was really little. Now I am seven, but I am still the youngest kid in Ms. Colman's class. (I skipped into first grade early.) I guess I will always be the youngest in my class.

I leaned over the pizza to see what Natalie was doing. She had carefully spread paper pepperoni over half of it.

"Now," said Nancy Dawes, "let's put extra cheese on one quarter of the pizza." (Nancy is one of my two best friends.)

"And let's put olives on the last quarter," suggested Hannie Papadakis. (She is my other best friend.) Hannie and Nancy and I are lucky to be together in Ms. Colman's class. Unluckily, I cannot sit with Hannie and Nancy. This is because I wear glasses. I sit in the front row so I can see better. Hannie and Nancy get to sit together in the back row.

"Not olives!" I shrieked. "Olives are gross!"

"Indoor voice," Ms. Colman reminded me gently.

Sometimes it is so hard to behave in school. It was especially hard on Paper Pizza Day. Paper Pizza Day was a Friday, and I was excited about Saturday. On Saturday my daddy was going to buy a van for his family, which is huge. He invited my brother, Andrew, and me to come with him.

"Today is Paper Pizza Day," I sang, "and tomorrow is Van Day!"

"Karen," said Ms. Colman, "will you come to my desk for a moment, please?" I left my pizza partners. I walked slowly to Ms. Colman. "What are you supposed to be doing now?" she asked me.

"Drawing a picture of our pizza," I answered. "And not talking."

"Right. Do you think you can calm down a little?"

"Yes," I said. I returned to my group. I did calm down, even though I thought a lot about Van Day at my father's house.

Ms. Colman is sooooo nice.

Only One Ms. Colman

My brother, Andrew, and I live at *two* houses. (Andrew is four, going on five.) We live at my father's house, which is as huge as his family. That is why I call it the big house. But mostly we live at my mother's house. I call that the little house.

Did you guess that the reason Andrew and I live at two houses is because Mommy and Daddy are divorced? If you did, you are right. But there is more to the story. Since I like telling stories, I will tell you the true story about my two families.

Once upon a time, Mommy and Daddy and Andrew and I lived together in the big house in Stoneybrook, Connecticut. Then Mommy and Daddy got divorced. Mommy moved into a little house nearby. She brought Andrew and me with her. Daddy stayed in the big house. (He had grown up there.) After awhile, Mommy and Daddy both got married again. But not to each other. Mommy married Seth. He is my stepfather. Daddy married Elizabeth. She is my stepmother. That is how Andrew and I got two families.

See, at the little house live Mommy and Seth and Andrew and I. And also Rocky and Midgie, Seth's cat and dog. Oh, and Emily Junior, my rat. But Andrew and I do not live there all the time. Every other weekend, and on some holidays and vacations, we live at the big house. There are lots of people in my big-house family. There are Daddy and Elizabeth and Andrew and I. There are also Elizabeth's four children. They are my stepbrothers and stepsister. Charlie and Sam go to high school. David Michael is seven like me. But we do not go to the same school. (David Michael goes to Stoneybrook Elementary. I go to a private school called Stoneybrook Academy.) Kristy is my stepsister. She is thirteen. I just love having a big sister. Especially one who is such a good baby-sitter. I also have a little sister. She is two and a half years old and her name is Emily Michelle. (I named my rat after her.) Daddy and Elizabeth adopted Emily. She came from a faraway country called Vietnam. When Emily came to stay, someone else moved to the big house — Nannie. Nannie is Elizabeth's mother, so she is my stepgrandmother. Plus, there are pets at the big house. They are Shannon, David Michael's puppy; Boo-Boo, Daddy's fat old tiger cat; and Goldfishie and Crystal Light the Second, two goldfish.

I have special nicknames for Andrew and me. I call us Andrew Two-Two and Karen Two-Two. (I did not think up the "two-

two" part of the names myself. I got that from the title of a book Ms. Colman read to our class. The book was called *Jacob Two-Two Meets the Hooded Fang*.) I call us two-twos because we have two of so many things. I have two bicycles, one at each house. I have two stuffed cats. (Moosie lives at the big house, Goosie lives at the little house.) Andrew and I have books and toys and clothes at each house. I even have a little-house best friend and a big-house best friend. Nancy Dawes lives next door to Mommy. Hannie Papadakis lives across the street and one house down from Daddy. Nancy and Hannie and I call ourselves the Three Musketeers. We have pledged that we will be friends 4-ever.

Most of the time, I feel lucky to be a two-two. But sometimes being a two-two is hard. After all, I do not have two of *every-thing*. I only have one pair of roller skates — which I am always forgetting and leaving behind at one of my houses. And I only had one Tickly, my special blanket.

I always used to forget Tickly, too. Finally I had to cut my blanket in half, so I could have a piece at each house. Also, when I am at the big house, I miss my little-house family. And when I am at the little house, I miss my big-house family.

That is why I am glad there is only one Ms. Colman. I could not imagine having another teacher. Ms. Colman is gigundo wonderful.

The Substitute

Monday morning. The weekend was over. Andrew and I had had lots of fun helping Daddy pick out a new van. (We were not his only helpers, though. Elizabeth, Kristy, David Michael, and Emily had joined us on Van Day.) Now Nancy and I were on our way to school. We usually ride together. Mrs. Dawes was driving us.

"When do you think we will get to make our pizzas?" Nancy wondered aloud.

"I don't know. Let's ask Ms. Colman this morning," I replied.

But Ms. Colman never came to school.

Instead, a substitute came. Ms. Colman was . . . sick.

Some kids like to have substitute teachers. Not me. I only like Ms. Colman. I was very sad. Our class would have to spend the day with somebody named Miss Pettig.

Miss Pettig was sitting at Ms. Colman's desk when Nancy and I reached our classroom. I knew her name was Miss Pettig because of the message she had written on our blackboard:

GOOD MORNING,
BOYS AND GIRLS!
MY NAME IS MISS PETTIG!

Well, for heaven's sake. The message looked like it had been written for babies. The letters were huge and round. Didn't Miss Pettig know that some people in our class can even read cursive already?

Nancy and I tiptoed into the room.

Miss Pettig saw us right away. "Good

morning," she said loudly. "My name is Miss Pettig. What are your names?"

"Nancy," mumbled Nancy.

"Karen," I mumbled.

"That's just fine," boomed Miss Pettig. "I am going to make a name tag for each of you. Then I will know your names all day."

"We have to wear *name* tags?" squeaked Nancy.

"We can make our own," I said.

I guess Miss Pettig did not hear us. She made the name tags anyway. She attached them to our fronts with big safety pins.

Later, when the bell rang, Miss Pettig stood up. "Hello, boys and girls," she said. "I am your substitute teacher." (Duh.) "Who can read what I wrote on the blackboard?"

I glanced at Ricky Torres, who sits next to me. (He wears glasses, too.) Everyone in our room could read what was written on the board. Ricky and I shrugged at each other.

Nobody did anything, so Miss Pettig smiled at us. "You must all be very shy," she said. (I have never been called shy before.) "All right. I will read it to you." Miss Pettig made her voice even louder. " 'Good morning, boys and girls! My name is Miss Pettig!' That is what I wrote on the board. I am sure some of you are wondering where Ms. Colman is. She is not feeling well today. But she will be back tomorrow."

Oh, thank goodness.

Here are some of the things we did with Miss Pettig on Monday:

We listened to her read a picture book called *We Help Mommy*. (Ms. Colman reads us big, long books like *Mr. Popper's Penguins*.)

We did a worksheet. We had to cross out the things that did not belong. We used to do cross-out worksheets in *kindergarten*. (Ms. Colman gives us neat projects, like paper pizzas.)

We colored pictures of a farm. All of our pictures looked the same. Miss Pettig told us which crayon to use for each part. (Ms. Colman lets us make things whatever color we want.)

The only good thing about Monday was that it ended.

The Surprising Awful Announcement

On Tuesday morning, Nancy and I ran through the hallway in school. We are supposed to *walk* in the halls, but Nancy and I were in a hurry. We had to make sure that Ms. Colman had really come back. So we ran to our classroom. Then we stopped short.

"Cross your fingers," I whispered to Nancy.

When our fingers were crossed, we peeped around the doorway.

The room was empty.

Yea!

We knew Ms. Colman was back. She almost never comes into our room until just before the bell rings.

Nancy and I waited for Hannie. When she arrived, the three of us sat quietly at our desks. "We do not want to give Ms. Colman a headache," I said.

At last, someone tall entered the room.

"Ms. Colman!" I cried happily.

Ms. Colman smiled. (She also said, "Indoor voice, Karen.")

The bell rang. Tuesday had begun. Ms. Colman sat at her desk. She looked a little tired. She must have caught the flu or something. After she took attendance, she stood up. "Class," she began. "I have an announcement to make."

I turned around and looked eagerly at Hannie and Nancy. We just love Ms. Colman's Surprising Announcements. She is always making them, and they are usually fun.

But this one was awful.

"Class," said Ms. Colman, "I have to tell you something. When I was absent yesterday, I went to the doctor. And the doctor says I need to have an operation. It isn't serious. But I will have to miss about a month of school."

Everyone began talking.

"An operation!" exclaimed Natalie.

"Are you going to the hospital?" Bobby asked.

"Are you coming back?" I cried.

"I will have the operation in the hospital," said Ms. Colman. "I will stay there for a week. After that, I can rest at home. And then I will come back to school. While I'm gone, you will have a substitute teacher."

"Miss Pettig?" asked Ricky. He shuddered.

"No. Somebody different. I hope you will like her."

I hoped so, too. Then I realized that nobody could be worse than Miss Pettig.

"Unfortunately," said Ms. Colman, "we will have to wait until I come back before we have our pizza party. But that will give us something to look forward to, won't it? A special class party."

How could I look forward to a party when Ms. Colman was going to go to the hospital? When she was going to have an operation?

I decided that this was the worst day of my life.

When school ended, I walked sadly to Ms. Colman's desk. "I wish you didn't have to go into the hospital," I told her.

"Me, too."

"I don't want you to go away."

"I don't want to go away, either. But I have to. I have to get well. It will only be a month, Karen. Four and a half weeks. Then I will be back."

I gave Ms. Colman a big good-bye hug.

A month seemed like forever.

Promises

I was not very happy that afternoon.

When Midgie nudged my knee with his cold nose, I shouted, "Cut that out!"

When Rocky went tearing through the house and ran across my feet, I shouted, "Stop that! Do you hear me?"

When Andrew asked me if I would play with him, I said, "Shut up! That is the fourth time you have asked me to play with you. Leave me alone!"

"Mom-meeeee!" wailed Andrew.

Mommy came into the kitchen. "Karen,"

she said, "please apologize to Andrew."

"Sorry," I said.

"For . . . ?" asked Mommy.

"Sorry for being cross and for telling you to shut up."

"Okay," said Andrew. But he was crying a little.

"Karen, why are you so angry this afternoon?" Mommy wanted to know.

"I just am. That's all."

"Are you angry because Ms. Colman is leaving?"

"NO!" I stomped upstairs to my room.

I stayed in my room until suppertime. Then I went downstairs long enough to eat dinner. I hardly talked at all during dinner. (That was not like me. Usually I talk, talk, talk. Seth calls me his chatterbox. That would make sense if boxes could talk.)

After dinner, I went right back to my room.

I closed the door.

I felt like being alone with Goosie and

Tickly. But a few minutes later I heard a *knock, knock* on my door.

I hoped Andrew was not out there. If he asked me just *one more time* to play with him I would —

"Karen?" It was Mommy.

"Come in," I said.

Mommy and Seth both came in. They sat on my bed. I sat between them.

"Do you want to talk about Ms. Colman?" asked Mommy.

"I don't know." I thought for a moment. Then I said, "I do not like it when people go away. Or animals."

"That can be hard," agreed Seth.

"It seems like someone is always going away. You and Daddy got divorced," I said to Mommy. "Amanda Delaney moved to a new town. Nannie had to go to the hospital for awhile. Louie died." (Louie was David Michael's first dog.) "And Crystal Light died." (She was the goldfish I had before I got Crystal Light the Second.)

"Those were not good times," said

Mommy. "But think of this. You are still here. You survived all those things. And Ms. Colman is coming back, you know."

"Promise," I said.

"We cannot *promise*," Seth told me.

"What if something goes wrong?" I asked.

"I think everything will be okay," said Mommy gently. She stroked my hair. "Remember how worried you were when Nannie went to the hospital? And then she got well and she came home. In time for Christmas."

I nodded. "I remember."

"Another thing," said Seth. "Just because Ms. Colman is in the hospital, does not mean you have to be out of touch with her. You could send her get-well cards."

"I could call her on the phone!" I exclaimed.

I felt better. But just a teensy bit better.

Karen's New Teacher

On Wednesday, Nancy and I rode to school together. Mommy drove us.

"What do you think she will be like?" asked Nancy, on the way.

"The substitute? I hope she will be like Ms. Colman," I answered.

"No one could be like Ms. Colman," said Nancy.

"I know. I was just hoping."

When we reached Stoneybrook Academy, Nancy and I tiptoed along the hallway again. We peeked into our room.

A lady was sitting at Ms. Colman's desk. "She looks mean," I whispered to Nancy. "Yeah."

The lady's hair was gray. So were her clothes. Ms. Colman wears bright, cheerful colors. And she does not have one single gray hair. (Even though grown-ups sometimes say to me, "Karen! You are giving me gray hair!")

"I guess we better go in," I said.

Nancy and I entered our classroom. The lady did not look up. She was writing something. But she said, "Please take your seats. You may read or draw until the bell rings. No talking, please."

A few other kids were already there — Natalie, Hannie, and Pamela Harding, who is my enemy. None of them said a word. They looked scared.

Goodness. Ms. Colman is hardly ever sitting at her desk when we come to school. And she lets us run around and talk and do whatever we want until the bell rings. As long as we do not hurt anything. Or each other.

At least our new substitute did not pin name tags on our fronts.

When the bell rang, the gray lady stood up. "Good morning," she said. (She did not smile.) "My name is Mrs. Hoffman. I will be your teacher until Ms. Colman comes back. In my classroom, we do not talk unless we raise our hands." How silly. This was not Mrs. Hoffman's room. It belonged to Ms. Colman. "Also," Mrs. Hoffman went on, "you will be seated in alphabetical order. I will tell you where to sit. You may not change your seats after that."

Alphabetical order! Ms. Colman had never seated us that way.

But Mrs. Hoffman did.

When we had finished moving around, I was still in the front row (since *Brewer* begins with a B). But Natalie and Ricky were sitting toward the back. I knew they would have trouble seeing the blackboard. And Hannie and Nancy were not sitting together anymore. Ms. Colman always let them sit together. Hannie looked like she wanted to cry.

Pamela Harding raised her hand.

"Yes?" said Mrs. Hoffman.

"I just want to thank you for changing our seats," said Pamela. She was sitting in her new place with her hands folded on the desk. "This makes much more sense. I think it is a very good idea."

Do you understand why I do not like Pamela?

"Thank you," Mrs. Hoffman replied. She checked the seating chart she had made. "Let me see. You are Pamela Harding, correct?"

"Correct. And I love rules."

That is not true! Pamela does not like rules at all.

"Wonderful. Rules are important," said Mrs. Hoffman.

I wanted to turn around and see

how Hannie was doing. But I decided I better not. I would probably be breaking a rule.

I thought of a new name for my new teacher. She was Hatey Hoffman.

★★★ and XXX

I was writing answers in my arithmetic workbook. I just love finishing pages in workbooks. I was glad that Hatey Hoffman had not said, "Boys and girls, we have a new rule: No workbooks!"

While we worked on our arithmetic, Hatey Hoffman was busy with something of her own. She was sitting at Ms. Colman's desk. She was writing on a big piece of posterboard. Sometimes she used a ruler to make lots of straight lines. Then she would write some more.

I finished my workbook pages. I was not sure what to do next. The other kids were still working. And Hatey Hoffman was still drawing lines and writing. She looked up and saw me sitting at my desk, doing nothing.

"Karen," she said, "please concentrate on your work."

"But I already — " I started to say. Then I remembered the raising-your-hand rule. I stopped talking. I raised my hand.

"Yes?" said Hatey Hoffman.

"I have finished my work," I said proudly.

"Then you may read silently. In my class, we never just sit."

"Oh." (I think I blushed.)

I pulled a copy of *The Story of Doctor Dolittle* out of my desk. I read until Hatey Hoffman said, "Math is over. Please put away your workbooks. Then I want everyone to face front. Eyes on the blackboard."

My friends and I put away our books.

We watched our new teacher tape the chart she had made to the blackboard.

"This is our class Chore Chart," announced Hatey Hoffman. "You can see that your names are written in a list down the left side of the chart. Next to each name, I have posted a chore. Your job will be to complete your chore before the end of the day. Tomorrow, the chores will change. They will change every day. So each morning, be sure to check the chart. Then be sure to do your chore. Every time you do those things, I will put a star by your name. If you do not check the chart and do your chore, I will put an X by your name."

Pamela raised her hand. "Mrs. Hoffman, what are the stars and X's for?" she wanted to know. She pretended to look very interested.

"I am glad you asked," replied Hatey Hoffman. "At the end of our month together, anyone who has earned fifteen or more stars will get . . . " (Well, *this* sounded

CHORE CHART

Karen Brewer........Clean sink a
Rickey Torres.........Clean eras
Nancy Dawes.....Collect H
Hannie Papad.....Water pla
Pamela........Clean guinea p
Billy........Feed guin
Ha

interesting. Maybe we would get a book or a toy.) ". . . will get," continued our new teacher, "a certificate."

Boo. A certificate is just a piece of paper.

I squinted my eyes to read what was written next to my name on the chart. (I had forgotten to put on my glasses. Ms. Colman would have reminded me.) Next to "Karen Brewer" was written "Clean sink area." Double boo. In the back of our classroom is a sink. We use it to wash our hands, to fill the watering can for our plants, to rinse out paintbrushes, and things like that. The sink is a horrible mess by the end of each school day.

Now I would have to clean it.

When school was over, I went to the back of the room. I almost ran. Then I remembered that Hatey Hoffman had a walking rule. I wiped up the sink. I polished it with paper towels. I thought it looked pretty good.

Across the room, Pamela was doing her chore. She was cleaning out Hootie's cage.

(Hootie is our guinea pig.) Cleaning his cage is a disgusting job. But Pamela did it anyway. She did not complain. When she had finished, she said to Hatey Hoffman, "Thank you so much for trusting me to clean Hootie's cage."

Oh, barf.

The Dunce

The next day, I tried to get to school later than usual. I did not want to sit around with Hatey Hoffman, waiting for the bell to ring. But Seth was driving Nancy and me to school, and he could not leave late.

"Here we go," I said glumly to Nancy. We had reached our classroom. We had peeked in and seen Hatey sitting at Ms. Colman's desk.

"Yeah," said Nancy. "Talk to you at lunchtime."

Nancy went to her desk. I went to mine.

"Good morning, girls," said Hatey.

"Good morning," replied Nancy.

"Good morning, Ha — I mean, good morning, Mrs. Hoffman," I said.

"Please read or draw silently."

I got out *The Story of Doctor Dolittle* again. I read and read. I came to a funny part and I started laughing.

"Hey, Ricky!" I cried. "Listen to this!" Then I remembered that Ricky did not sit next to me anymore. I also remembered that we were not supposed to talk.

Hatey Hoffman checked the seating chart. She found my name. (I guess she had forgotten who I was since yesterday.) "Karen Brewer," she said in a very loud voice. "No talking before the bell rings. And no talking unless you raise your hand. Did you understand those rules when I explained them?"

"Yes," I said quietly. I could tell that everyone was staring at me.

"All right, then."

The bell rang and our school day began. Hatey Hoffman said, "The first thing we will do is exercise our brains. I will give you a surprise spelling quiz."

"A sur*prise* quiz!" I exclaimed.

"Karen," said Hatey Hoffman warningly. She shook her head. Then she said, "Who is our paper-passer today?"

I looked at the Chore Chart. *I* was!

"I am!" I shouted.

"Karen Brewer. Will you *please* remember to raise your hand? What gets into you? Where are your best manners? Now be quiet!"

I passed out the papers silently. I wondered what *best manners* were.

Hatey Hoffman did not yell at me again until the afternoon. It was science time. We were reading aloud from our books. This was really boring. Ms. Colman lets us do experiments.

My mind wandered. I began to doodle

on the page that was headed *The Sun, the Moon, and the Stars*. I noticed that Leslie was doodling, too. (Leslie is one of Pamela's good friends.)

"Karen Brewer!" yelled Hatey Hoffman for the second time that day. She peered down at my desk. "Drawing in your book," she said. "All right. I have had enough. Please go stand in the corner for ten minutes."

Stand in the *corner?* I have never had to do that. Ms. Colman never tells any of us to stand in the corner. And what about Leslie? She was doodling, too. But Hatey had not seen her. That was because she had been watching *me* all day. She was just waiting for me to make another mistake.

When ten minutes had gone by, Hatey said I could return to my seat. On my way there, I passed Pamela's desk.

"Dunce," she whispered.

I knew I could not answer her. I would

get into trouble again. I did not even say anything when Hatey let Pamela pass out our homework sheets. That was *my* job. I guess Hatey thought I deserved an X that day. How unfair.

Two Straight Lines

"Please practice lining up," said Hatey Hoffman.

Practice lining up? Ms. Colman asked us to practice lots of things. She asked us to practice our cursive writing. She asked us to practice our arithmetic facts, and counting by twos and threes and fives and tens. She asked us to practice the Golden Rule. (The Golden Rule is: *Do unto others as you would have others do unto you.* I really have no idea what that means. Hannie says it means be nice to everybody.) Anyway, Ms.

Colman often asked our class to practice something. But she had never said, "Practice lining up." She did not have to. We have known how to line up since we were in preschool.

Pamela raised her hand. "Excuse me?" she said to Hatey. "You want us to practice making a line?"

"Exactly," Hatey replied. "You be the leader, Pamela."

Pamela stood up. She walked to the doorway. Everybody else jumped to their feet. We raced to stand behind Pamela. We made a lot of noise. (Ricky knocked over his chair. This was not the first time it had happened.)

"Just as I thought," said Hatey. She looked at the scraggly line we had formed. "Back to your seats, please."

We clattered to our desks. (Ricky knocked over his chair again.)

"From now on," said Hatey, "you will line up in two lines like ladies and gentlemen. Girls, you will line up along the chalkboard. You will line up in alphabetical order according to your last name. Boys, you will line up next to the girls, in the same manner. You will walk to your lines and *stay* in line. When we walk through the halls, we will stay in two straight lines. And there will be no talking."

No talking is Hatey's favorite rule. I wonder why she does not like to hear our voices. I just love to talk.

Later on Friday morning, we went to gym class. We walked down the hallway in our two straight lines. (I was the leader of my line. Guess who was right behind me. Nancy Dawes.)

Hatey walked ahead of our two lines. So she did not see when two fourth-grade kids who were passing by stopped and pointed. Then they laughed.

When we walked to the cafeteria for lunch, we had to walk in our lines again. This time three fifth-grade girls passed by Hatey. They looked at our lines. Then one of them said, "Just like in that baby book

Madeline. The children had to walk in two straight lines. Only they were all *girls*."

Even though she said this very softly, we could hear her. She made us mad. Especially the boys. But we could not say, "Meanie-mo!" because of Hatey's no-talking rule. So we made angry faces and kept on walking.

Here is how mad we were. We were so gigundoly mad that even Pamela Harding was mad. She did not like walking in two straight lines. No other kids in Stoneybrook Academy had to do that. Everyone stared at us. Even the teachers.

After recess that day, Hatey Hoffman led us back to our classroom in two straight lines.

I forgot the no-talking rule.

"Hey!" I said to Nancy. "The *prin*cipal is staring at us."

Hatey turned around fast. "Karen Brewer," she said. "Where are your best manners? Why can't you remember rules? This weekend, you will have an extra homework assignment. You will write an essay called, 'Why I Should Follow School Rules.' The essay must be fifty words long."

TRIPLE BOO.

But one good thing happened that afternoon. Pamela did not do her chore. She did not do it on purpose. She did not say a word when Hatey gave her an X. Pamela was still mad.

School Rules

"She is my worst teacher ever," I said. "And I hate, hate, hate her!"

"Karen, please do not say you hate anyone," said Daddy. "*Hate* is not a very nice word."

"Well, Mrs. Hoffman is not a very nice teacher," I replied. But I was glad I had not said that my nickname for my new teacher was Hatey.

It was Friday evening. Mommy had driven Andrew and me to the big house for the weekend. Now my brother and I were eating dinner with Daddy, Elizabeth, Nannie, Kristy, Charlie, Sam, David Michael, and Emily. I was telling everyone how awful Hatey Hoffman was.

"She has rules, rules, rules," I went on. "We have to do everything in alphabetical order. And she is *so* strict."

"What's alphabetical order?" asked Andrew.

"It's boring," I replied. "Plus, we have to walk in two straight lines, and we can never talk, and nobody likes the Chore Chart, and — "

"Karen," said Kristy, "is there anything good about Mrs. Hoffman?"

"No," I said.

After dinner, I went upstairs. I sat down at the table in my bedroom. I was going to begin the composition on school rules. It was not due until Monday morning. But I wanted to write it before I went to bed that night. I was not going to let it hover around and spoil my weekend.

I thought for a moment. Then I wrote

down the title of the essay: *Why I Should Follow School Rules.* Did those count as the first six words of the essay? I wondered. Or would Hatey start counting after the title? Then I wondered if *I* counted as a word. It is only one letter long. Then I wondered if Hatey wanted *exactly* fifty words. What if my composition was fifty-two words or something? Would I have to write it again?

I could not answer any of my questions.

Instead, I made up a song about Hatey. I sung it to the tune of "Old MacDonald Had a Farm." Here is how it went: *"Hatey Hoffman had a class. H-A-T-E-Y. And to her class she was quite mean. H-A-T-E-Y. Oh, we hate, hate Hatey. Yes, we hate, hate Hatey. Hatey Hoffman, Hatey Hoffman, Hatey Hoffman, Hatey. Hatey Hoffman had a class. H-A-T-E-Y."*

Knock, knock.

Uh-oh. Someone was at my door.

Tricking Mrs. Hoffman

Had I been singing *very* loudly? I was not sure. But I *was* sure that if Daddy had heard the song, he would be cross with me.

Knock, knock. "Karen? It's Sam. Can I come in?"

Phew! Sam was safe. He would not care about my song. He would probably like it. Sam likes jokes and goofing on people and making funny phone calls.

"Come in!" I yelled.

Sam came into my room. He closed the door behind him. Then he sat on my bed. "Working on your composition?" he asked.

"Sort of," I replied. "I wrote down the title. Then I made up a song. Want to hear it?" Sam nodded, so I sang "Hatey Hoffman Had a Class."

Sam laughed. Then he said, "Too bad you can't write your composition about substitutes."

"How come?" I asked.

"Well, think what you could write about. You could write about how awful substitutes are, and how they — "

"Are *all* substitutes awful?" I asked.

Sam looked thoughtful. Then he said, "No. . . . But they are fun to trick. Me and my friends trick our real teachers sometimes." (I could never, ever trick Ms. Colman. She is much too nice.) "But substitutes are much more fun. Once, Jeremy and I . . ."

Sam talked and talked. While he talked, I got an idea. As soon as Sam left my room, I made a phone call. I called Hannie.

"Hi," I said. "It's me. And you would not be*lieve* what I just thought of."

"Probably not," agreed Hannie. "What?"

"We should trick Mrs. Hoffman."

"Us? Trick her? Are you crazy?"

"Not just you and me. The whole class. Nobody likes Mrs. Hoffman now. Not even Pamela Harding."

"But if we trick her, we will get in trouble."

"I don't think so," I told Hannie. "What is Mrs. Hoffman going to do? Send *all* of us to the principal's office? No way. She will look like a horrible teacher if she does that."

"Hmm," said Hannie. "I don't know. I do not think we should trick teachers."

"But this is not just any teacher," I reminded her. "This is *Mrs. Hoffman*."

"Yeah. . . . All right. What could we do to her?"

I smiled. I tried to remember the tricks that Sam said he had played. "Oh, there are so many possibilities," I replied.

Hannie and I talked until Kristy yelled up the stairs, "Who is being a phone-hog? I need to make a call."

"Okay," I shouted back. I told Hannie I had to hang up. Then I returned to my composition. "Why I should follow school rules," I murmured. "So I won't get in trouble and have extra homework," I said. But I knew I could not write that. I could not write anything I *really* wanted to say.

After lots of thinking and lots of writing and lots of cross-outs, I wrote: *School rules are very, very, very important. They help keep our school running smoothly. They really, really do. If a nice, nice visitor comes to Stoneybrook Academy, he (or this person could be a she) would want to see an orderly school. Since I am very, very proud of my school, I want it to look nice. Thank you.*

I hoped the length would be okay with Hatey. I figured it would be. Not counting the title, it was 59 words long.

Now — two whole days without Hatey Hoffman.

The First Trick

"Okay, everybody. Come here! I have an idea," I announced.

Recess was just about the only time my classmates and I did not have to be in alphabetical order. We did not have to be in lines, either.

Everyone ran to me. Sometimes when I announce that I have an idea, the kids just groan and say, "Not another one." But they figured that this idea had something to do with Mrs. Hoffman. And they were as desperate as I was.

"What is it?" cried Ricky and Natalie and the twins, Terri and Tammy.

Even Pamela said, "Yeah, what is it?"

"We," I began, "are going to get back at Mrs. Hoffman. We are going to play tricks on her."

"I'm not," said Pamela.

"What kind of tricks?" Bobby wanted to know.

"Nothing *too* awful," I replied. "Just sort of pesty. Pesty enough to give Mrs. Hoffman a hard time. *She* has not been very nice to *us* so far."

"Okay, okay," said Bobby. "What kind of tricks?"

"There are lots we can play," I told my classmates. "We just have to decide which one to play first." I talked about Sam's tricks.

By the time recess was over, we had a plan. But we did not have Pamela. She said she did not want to trick Mrs. Hoffman. Then she walked away.

Oh, well.

The bell rang. My friends and I walked to Mrs. Hoffman. Silently, we formed our two straight lines. We walked through the halls to our room. The older kids were probably staring at us again. But I did not notice. I was thinking about what was going to happen that afternoon. I was excited. And scared.

When we reached our classroom, I snagged Pamela.

"Don't you want to — " I whispered.

"No!" hissed Pamela. She hurried to her seat.

I wished Pamela would be part of our trick. But if she did not want to join us, that was okay. It was sort of too bad, though. Pamela did not even know that at exactly two o'clock something was going to happen.

"Everybody in your seats, please," said Mrs. Hoffman.

I looked at her. I looked at her gray hair and her gray clothes and her frown. And I thought of something. I realized that I had never seen Mrs. Hoffman smile. Not once. Even Miss Pettig had smiled at us. I wished Miss Pettig could have been our substitute. A month of baby books and name tags would have been much, *much* better than Hatey Hoffman.

"Take out your science books," said Hatey.

From 1:30 to 1:45, we took turns reading aloud. At 1:45, Hatey said, "Okay. That is enough. Now please close your books. Then answer the questions I have written on the board."

The paper-passer passed out paper. Nobody said a word. (Except for Hootie. He was whistling in his cage.) My friends and I wrote busily. We watched the clock on the wall. The little hand was on the two and the big hand was *click, clicking* toward the twelve. When the time was exactly two o'clock . . .

BANG!

Every kid in my class knocked his (or her) science book to the floor.

"Aughhh!" shrieked Pamela.

Hatey Hoffman jumped a mile. "Pick up those books at once!" she ordered. (We picked them up.) "I will not have such behavior in my classroom! Where are your best manners?" Hatey yelled for a few more minutes. But that was all she did.

So what? I thought. I began thinking of the next way to trick Hatey.

Underwear

A few days later, Mrs. Hatey Hoffman gave our class another spelling test. Only this one was not a surprise. She had told us about it right after she finished yelling at us for dropping our books on the floor. So we had had plenty of time to study for it.

But none of us studied except Pamela. This was because of our next trick.

On the day of the quiz, Hatey told us to clear off our desks. This was a clue. It meant that the paper-passer should pass out paper. Hannie did her job. She gave me four pieces of paper. I took one and handed the rest to the person behind me. I could not look at Hannie. If I had looked at her, we would have laughed.

When everyone had a piece of paper, Hatey said, "The first word is *throw*. Throw. John can throw the ball. Throw."

Hatey paused. She waited for us to begin writing. But my friends and I just sat in our chairs. Except Pamela. She scribbled something on her paper. She would not look at anybody else. When she finished writing, she folded her hands on her desk. She looked at Hatey. (I noticed that she did not smile.)

After a moment, Hatey continued, "The second word is *picture*. Picture. He took my picture with a camera. Picture."

Once again, no one moved except Pamela.

Hatey frowned. But she gave out all twenty spelling words. When Pamela had finished taking the quiz, Mrs. Hoffman took her paper. Then she collected the blank pages from the rest of us. She did not say anything.

Were we in trouble? I could not tell. I knew we had done something that was wrong. But Hatey was not yelling.

Later, just before it was time to line up to go to the cafeteria, Hatey handed back our papers. I looked at mine. At the top was a fat, red ZERO. I had never, ever gotten a zero in school. In fact, I almost always get one hundreds.

I tried to see what Pamela's score was, but Pamela stuffed her test paper quickly into her desk. I found out in the cafeteria, though. We all did. At lunchtime Pamela waited until Hatey had gone to the teachers' room. Then she put her hands on her hips.

"Guess what," she said crossly.

"You got a one hundred on your quiz," said Tammy.

"No, Miss Smarty," replied Pamela. "Mrs. Hoffman gave me a forty percent.

Forty! What was the point of taking that stupid test? I should have done what you guys did. . . . Mrs. Hoffman is awful."

I knew Pamela was on my side then. But I was still surprised by what happened that afternoon. We were supposed to be completing a science worksheet. The room was silent except for Hootie. After awhile, though, I thought I heard another sound. A humming. Sure enough, someone was softly humming the tune to the "Underwear" song, the song that begins, *"Underwear, underwear, how I itch in my woolly underwear."*

Pamela was humming! Slowly, the rest of us joined in. Our room sounded like a swarm of crickets on a summer night.

Did Hatey tell us to be quiet? No.

Did she ask us what had happened to our best manners? No.

Did she yell? No.

But at the end of the day, she gave us extra homework. We were supposed to complete some pages in our math workbook and our reading workbook. We were also supposed to write a 100-word composition. "You need practice," said Hatey. "Your work is sloppy."

It was Thursday. The composition was due Monday.

14

The Worst Teacher Ever

I spent most of the weekend working on my composition. My friends and I had thought about *not* writing the composition. But we did not want to get any more zeros. What would Ms. Colman think when she came back?

Besides, I had a great idea for my composition. Hatey had said we could write about anything. So this was the title of my composition: *The Worst Teacher Ever*. It was about a girl named Carrie who got a new teacher. The teacher was named Mrs. Hoffburger, and she was Carrie's worst teacher ever. She made Carrie and her friends walk around school in two straight lines. She would not let them talk — ever. Once, she made Carrie stand in the corner.

I checked my paper over three times before I copied it in ink. I made sure every word was spelled right. I wrote as neatly as I could, in cursive.

On Monday I handed *The Worst Teacher Ever* to Hatey.

On Wednesday, Hatey returned our compositions. She walked from desk to desk. As she gave back each paper, she would say, "Nice work," or, "Pay attention to your spelling." Mostly she said, "Your writing is sloppy."

When Hatey came to me, she placed my composition on my desk. But she did not say anything. She set her mouth in a line. I looked at the grade Hatey had written at the top of the paper. A big, red A. But she had not written any comment or made any notes.

Hmm. What did that mean?

The day went on. We went to the cafeteria. We played on the playground. We had science class and then some time to read. Just before the bell rang, Hatey got up from Ms. Colman's desk. She stood stiffly in front of my friends and me.

"Class," she began, "your compositions were quite sloppy — mostly. They were covered with eraser marks. Some of you even erased *holes* in your papers. Your handwriting was messy and hard to read. Several of you doodled in the margins. So I decided that it is time for you to learn to be neat. And the best way to be neat is to dress neatly. From now on, I expect every one of you to come to school dressed for learning, not for the playground. Nobody may wear jeans or sneakers. Girls may not wear pants."

Everyone groaned. I heard someone whisper, "I wonder if we could wear our slippers."

Hatey raised an eyebrow at us. We stopped talking.

How mean. *My* paper had not been sloppy. Hatey had not even needed to correct anything. So why did *I* have to stop wearing jeans and sneakers?

The next day, my friends and I wore our good clothes to school. (A fifth-grader asked us if it was class-picture day.) Nobody wore jeans. Nobody wore sneakers. The girls wore dresses or skirts. We could not do *any*thing at recess. So we stood around in a bunch.

We grumbled.

"I *hate* my shoes," said Ricky. "They pinch my toes."

"*I* hate my *dress*," said Natalie.

"What are we going to do?" asked Hannie.

Everyone looked at me.

"Don't look at me," I said. "I am out of ideas."

"But I'm not." Pamela Harding was grinning. "I have a great idea."

"*You* do?" Bobby was so surprised that he almost fell over, even though he was standing still. "*You* do?" he said again.

"What is it?" I asked.

"It's *this*."

Pamela began whispering, and we all leaned in to hear her better.

Backward Day

The next day, my friends and I followed Hatey's dressing rules again. The boys wore their good shirts and good pants and good shoes. The girls wore dresses or skirts or jumpers with party shoes.

As soon as we got to school, we ran to the bathrooms. We changed our clothes.

We put everything on backward.

"See?" I said to Nancy as we admired our outfits. (We were in the girls' room. We were looking at ourselves in the mirror.) "We are following all of Mrs. Hoffman's

rules. She said, 'No jeans.' She said, 'No sneakers.' She said, 'No pants for the girls.' And we are not wearing any of those things."

Nancy giggled. "What lovely ladies we are."

I was wearing a very fancy dress. It was supposed to button down the back. I had buttoned it down the front. And I had tied the sashes in a big bow — in front. Nancy was wearing a backward blouse and a backward skirt. She was also wearing a backward sweater. I had helped her button the sweater down her back.

We had both put our shoes on the wrong feet.

Just before we entered our classroom, I stopped. I turned my glasses upside down. Then I set them on my nose.

We walked into the room. (We held hands because we were a teensy bit scared.) But for once, Hatey was not there. About half of our classmates were, though. And, boy, did they look silly! Ricky was wearing a suit. The jacket and pants were fastened in the back. Hank Reubens was wearing a softball cap. The brim was facing the back.

"Mrs. Hoffman did not say, 'No hats,' " he told Nancy and me.

Natalie had combed all of her hair over her face. Then she had put on her glasses.

I looked around the room. Where was Pamela? This was her idea. If she did not show up, I would —

"Hello, everybody!" Pamela walked proudly through the doorway.

She was dressed as a bride. Her shoes were on the wrong feet. Her gown was on backward. (She had to carry the train in front of her.) And the veil completely covered her face. I do not know how she could see anything.

Everybody began to laugh.

But suddenly we stopped. The room grew silent.

Hatey Hoffman had arrived.

Guess what she did. She *laughed!* "I have

never seen a sillier looking class," she said. She laughed some more.

I was amazed. No yelling? No extra homework?

My friends and I were pretty quiet all morning.

But I was even more amazed that afternoon. I could not believe what happened when Hatey met our class at the end of recess.

The bell rang. My backward friends and I ran to the doorway. We formed our two straight lines. Hatey was waiting for us.

All of her clothes were on backward!

We walked silently through the halls. We entered our classroom. And then . . . *everybody* began to laugh.

Pamela raised her hand. "How do you like Backward Day?" she asked Mrs. Hoffman.

Mrs. Hoffman shook her head. "Did you ever do this for Ms. Colman?" She was still laughing.

I raised my hand. "We never had to," I replied.

"I see," said Mrs. Hoffman. Suddenly she looked serious. But not cross. "Why is that?"

"Because Ms. Colman does not have so many rules," I said. "We can behave ourselves without rules. We are pretty good at it."

"Okay," said Mrs. Hoffman. "Show me."

The Big Rock Candy Mountain

The first school day after Backward Day was *great*.

Guess what I noticed when I walked into our room — NO CHORE CHART. Mrs. Hoffman had taken it down. Even so, every single chore was done by the end of the day. (I cleaned Hootie's cage. I do not like the mess. But I like Hootie.)

When we came in that morning, we stopped talking. We walked silently to our desks. We got out our books and began to read.

Do you know what Mrs. Hoffman said? She said, "Natalie. Ricky. Why are you two sitting so far back? All glasses-wearers come to the front row." Then she said, "Hannie. Nancy. Why are you two sitting so far apart? Please move to the back row so you can be together."

Mrs. Hoffman changed our seats all around. We were back in our old places. Ricky was next to me. Hannie and Nancy were next to each other. Everyone was where they belonged.

The bell had not rung yet. So I pulled *Doctor Dolittle* out of my desk. My friends opened their books. The room was quiet again.

"Ahem," said Mrs. Hoffman. "Something is wrong. I do not hear any noise. School has not started yet. Why are you so quiet?"

I grinned. I put away *Doctor Dolittle*, even though I had reached a very funny part. I turned to Ricky. "Nice suit," I said.

"Nice dress," Ricky replied.

Everyone else was talking, too. But no one was running around. No chairs were knocked over. Nobody was fighting or throwing spitballs.

Mrs. Hoffman smiled at us. Then, slowly, her smile turned into a frown. She bent down. She looked at our feet. Then she straightened up.

"Boys and girls, you are awfully dressed up," she said. "I do not see any sneakers. I do not see any jeans. And all the girls are wearing dresses."

I raised my hand. "Mrs. Hoffman?" I said. "Could we wear our regular clothes tomorrow? I promise we will not erase any holes in our papers."

"You may wear your . . . regular clothes," replied Mrs. Hoffman.

"Thank you," I said.

The bell rang. Our day with Mrs. Hoffman began. She did not have to yell at anybody. She did not have to send anybody to the corner. Best of all, when we lined up to go to the cafeteria, Mrs. Hoffman raised her eyebrows.

"Why are you standing in two lines?" she asked us.

We formed one line. We walked down the hall. We were quiet and orderly.

Nobody made fun of us.

The afternoon went as well as the morning. The second day went as well as the first. And at the end of the second day, Mrs. Hoffman surprised us. She reached into Ms. Colman's closet. She pulled out a guitar.

I never knew Mrs. Hoffman could play the guitar.

But she could.

She taught us a new song. It was called "The Big Rock Candy Mountain." I liked the song a lot. (This made sense. I like to sing, and I like to eat candy.)

When we had learned all the words to the song, Mrs. Hoffman said, "Wonderful!

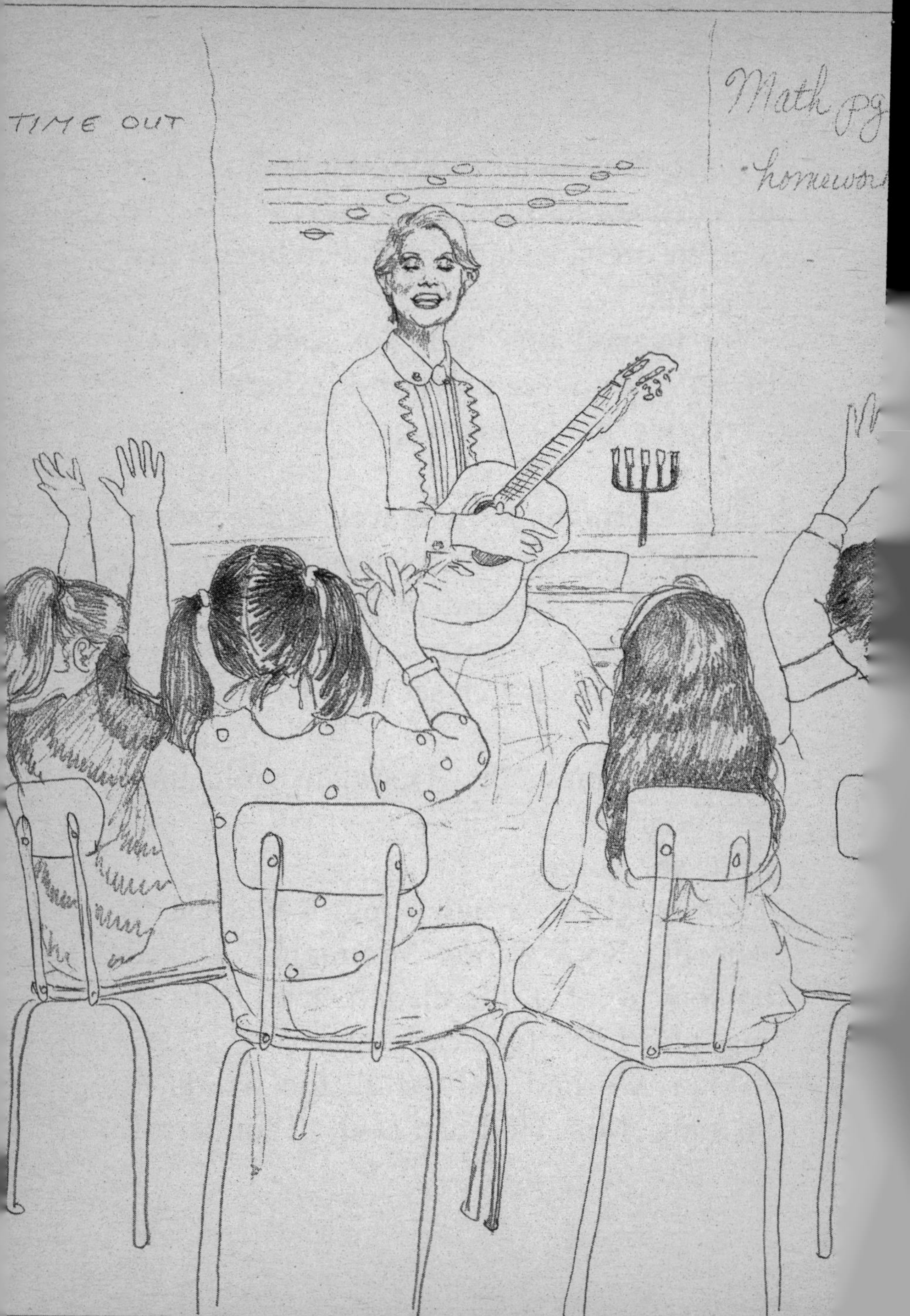
TIME OUT
Math pg

You are very nice singers. We will sing for fifteen minutes at the end of each day if you behave as well as you have been behaving."

I raised my hand. "Thank you," I said.

Mrs. Hoffman smiled. Then she said, "By the way, I certainly liked the sound of 'The Big Rock Candy Mountain' better than the sound of 'Underwear.' "

A Present for Mrs. Hoffman

One day, Mrs. Hoffman said, "Well, boys and girls, this will be our last week together. Ms. Colman will be back on Monday."

That was hard to believe. Ms. Colman had been away for *three and a half weeks*. Seven days from now, she would be sitting at her desk again.

I could not wait! Ms. Colman would be all well. School would be the same as before. Ms. Colman would read to us. She would make Surprising Announcements.

We would have our pizza party at last.

Then I realized something. I would miss Mrs. Hoffman's guitar. I would miss singing with Mrs. Hoffman at the end of the day.

At recess, I called to my classmates, "Come here for a sec!"

Everyone gathered around me. Pamela Harding joined them. She had not been *quite* so mean since Backward Day.

"Friday will be Mrs. Hoffman's last day," I said.

"Duh," replied Bobby. (He can be *so rude*.)

I ignored him. "I was thinking," I went on. "I will kind of miss singing 'The Big Rock Candy Mountain' after Mrs. Hoffman leaves."

"I will miss her guitar," said Ricky.

"I will miss Mrs. Hoffman," said Hannie.

"Maybe we could do something nice for her," said Nancy. "Maybe we could give her a going-away party. I bet she would like that."

"Yeah!" I cried. "We could have refreshments."

"We could sing," said Ricky.

"We could give Mrs. Hoffman a present," I added.

We were very busy the next few days. We talked to the room mothers. They said they would make punch and cake. They would buy napkins and stuff. They would bring everything to school on Friday afternoon. We could surprise our teacher.

"What about a present?" I asked my friends. It was Wednesday. We were on the playground. But we were not playing. We were talking about the party again. "We have only two days to buy her something."

"I know!" said Hannie. "Everyone should bring some money to school tomorrow."

"Right," agreed Nancy. "Then Karen can collect the money — "

"And I will buy the present after school," I finished. "Oh, but I will need someone to come with me. I don't want to choose all by myself."

"I will come with you," offered Ricky.

And he did. The next day, we collected almost *eight dollars*. When school was over, Mommy picked up Ricky and me. She drove us downtown. She drove us to the dime store. The dime store has very beautiful jewelry.

"Can you stay in the car, please?" I asked Mommy. "Ricky and I want to buy the present like grown-ups."

Mommy sat in the car. Ricky and I went into the store.

"The jewelry is over here," I said. I led Ricky to a big bin. It was filled with necklaces and bracelets and pins and earrings. Nearly everything was plastic. And gorgeous. We would probably have trouble making up our minds. We looked and looked.

Ricky held up a necklace made of red and white beads.

"Nope," I said.

I held up a pair of huge gold earrings.

"Nope," said Ricky.

Then we both reached for the same thing. A blue pin shaped like a flower. Ricky and I grinned at each other.

"Can we afford it?" I asked.

Ricky checked the price tag. "Yup," he replied.

So we bought the pin.

Good-bye, Mrs. Hoffman

On Thursday night I could hardly fall asleep. I was too excited. The next day, we would give Mrs. Hoffman her good-bye party. The party would be fun. Saying good-bye would not be fun. But on Monday Ms. Colman would be back! She would sit at her desk. She would remind me to use my indoor voice and to wear my glasses. Maybe she would make a Surprising Announcement.

The rest of my friends were excited, too. We had a little trouble thinking about our work. But we tried very hard to use our best manners. (Or to find our best manners after we had lost them.) We did all the chores that used to be on the Chore Chart. (I cleaned Hootie's cage again.) We lined up neatly. We did not talk in the hallway (much). And we almost always remembered to raise our hands. I thought this was amazing. We were keeping such a big secret. Actually, I was keeping two secrets. I had my own surprise to give Mrs. Hoffman after the party. But I would give it to her in private.

We were writing compositions in the afternoon, when I glanced at the door. There were the room mothers.

"They're he-ere!" I whispered to Ricky.

Mrs. Hoffman frowned at me. I think she was going to ask me what had happened to my best manners. But the room mothers came in then. One of them was holding a plate. The cake was on it.

"Surprise!" shouted Nancy and Hannie

and Ricky and Bobby and Natalie and Pamela and Tammy and Terri and I. "Surprise!"

Mrs. Hoffman certainly acted surprised. She jumped about a mile. Then she calmed down. She smiled. She looked at the cake. It was decorated with pink roses. In the middle was written: GOOD-BYE, MRS. HOFFMAN!

"Thank you very much," said Mrs. Hoffman. "Thank you, boys and girls."

I raised my hand. "Can we put away our compositions?" I asked.

Mrs. Hoffman laughed. "Of course you may."

We cleared our desks.

Mrs. Hoffman cut the cake. The room mothers passed a piece to everyone. Then they passed around cups of juice.

When we had finished eating, I said, "Let's play a game."

Mrs. Hoffman let us play Seven-up. After that, we divided into teams and played

Hangman on the blackboard. (My team lost.)

Then Mrs. Hoffman said, "How about one last song?"

She got out her guitar. We sang *two* last songs. First we sang "The Big Rock Candy Mountain." Then we taught Mrs. Hoffman the song about underwear. She said that this is her favorite part of the song: *"BVDs make me sneeze, when the breeze from the trees hits my knees!"*

Soon, only ten minutes were left until the bell would ring.

I nudged Ricky. "It's time," I said.

Ricky nodded. He reached into his desk. He pulled out the present we had bought at the dime store. It was wrapped in a gigundoly beautiful way. Ricky's father had wrapped it. He had used silver ribbon, which was a nice touch.

Ricky and I stepped to the front of the classroom. Ricky held the present toward Mrs. Hoffman. I said, "Mrs. Hoffman, this is for you."

Mrs. Hoffman opened her present. "Oh, it's perfect!" she exclaimed. She pinned on the blue flower. It looked really nice against her orange sweater. Then Mrs. Hoffman began to look serious. Ricky and I sat down. So did everyone else. "The day is almost over," said Mrs. Hoffman. "I just want you to know that you are one class I will never forget!"

Karen's Last Surprise

The party was over. Almost everyone had left our classroom. Even the room mothers. I was helping Mrs. Hoffman clean up the napkins and paper plates. (I had told Mommy I would be ten minutes late that afternoon.) Ricky was washing the blackboard. When he finished, he left.

The room was quiet.

"Mrs. Hoffman?" I said. "I have some homework for you."

Mrs. Hoffman looked puzzled. "You

don't owe me any homework, Karen," she said.

"Yes, I do." I opened my notebook. I took out a piece of paper. I handed it to Mrs. Hoffman. (It was some of my best work ever. It was my last surprise.)

Mrs. Hoffman looked at my paper. "A composition," she said. "Is this the one you were writing this afternoon?"

I shook my head. "Nope. I did this at home."

Mrs. Hoffman read the title. *"My New Teacher."*

"It's to take the place of this," I said. I held up *The Worst Teacher Ever*. Then I tore it in half. "I am really sorry," I said. "I am sorry for the things I wrote here, and I am sorry I called you Mrs. Hoffburger. It was nice of you to give me a good grade. But I would rather have a good grade on *My New Teacher*."

Mrs. Hoffman sat down. She read the new composition. It was about a girl named

Karen Brewer and her substitute teacher, Mrs. Hoffman. It told how Karen missed her old teacher, Ms. Colman, very much. And how she and her friends were confused by Mrs. Hoffman's rules. It said that Karen was used to a teacher who understood that she was the youngest one in the class. And who would remind her to use her indoor voice. And who had never sent her to stand in the corner.

It was seventy-nine words long.

"Do you know what?" I said to Mrs. Hoffman. "I sent Ms. Colman three get-well cards. She sent me a letter. Once, we talked on the phone. But I was still afraid she would not come back."

"And you did not want *me* to replace her," said Mrs. Hoffman with a smile.

"I did not want *anyone* to replace her."

"So you were afraid to give me a chance."

I nodded. "But I am glad about what happened on Backward Day," I said. "And I will miss your guitar. And singing songs in the afternoon. I will not forget those things."

"And I will *certainly* not forget you."

"Good-bye, Mrs. Hoffman," I said.

"Good-bye, Karen."

Hello, Ms. Colman!

Monday, Monday! It had come at last! It was almost as good as my birthday or Halloween. At breakfast, I could not sit still.

"Karen!" exclaimed Mommy. "You are acting like a Mexican jumping bean."

"Ms. Colman's coming back!" I replied.

I poked Andrew. He poked me. I poked him again. He poked me again.

Seth separated us.

"What if she does *not* come back?" I asked suddenly. I was sitting at the counter. (Andrew got to stay at the table.)

"I am pretty sure she will be back," said Mommy.

"What if she does *not* come back?" I said to Nancy on the way to school.

"I thought about that," replied Nancy.

"We better tiptoe to our room. We should keep our fingers crossed."

Nancy and I tiptoed all the way to our classroom. Our fingers were crossed. We said softly, "Please be back, please be back, please be back."

We looked into the room.

Empty!

"She's back!" cried Nancy.

Natalie came in. Then Hannie came in. Then Pamela arrived. Then Bobby and Tammy and Terri arrived.

And then . . . Ms. Colman walked through the door!

"Ms. Colman! Hello, Ms. Colman!" I cried. "You came back!"

I ran to my teacher. I hugged her.

Ms. Colman hugged me.

Soon everyone had crowded around Ms. Colman. We were one big hug.

"Are you all better?" asked Nancy.

"I'm all better," said Ms. Colman. "I feel fine."

"You do not look tired anymore," I told her.

"I had a long rest."

"What was the hospital like?" asked Natalie.

Well, for heaven's sake. Everyone knows that the hospital is no fun.

But Ms. Colman did not get impatient. She said, "It's a nice place to visit, but I would not want to live there."

We laughed. Then I said, "Did you get to watch the soaps on TV?"

"I could have watched them," Ms. Colman answered, "but . . . Karen, where are your glasses? What are you doing without them?"

"I forgot them," I said. (I had forgotten on purpose.) Then I yelled, "Hey, Ms. Colman!"

"Indoor voice, Karen," she reminded me.

I smiled. Everything was back to normal.

The other kids drifted away. Not me. I stood right by Ms. Colman's desk. I watched her take out the attendance book.

"I was afraid you would not come back," I said to her.

"Well, sometimes people go away and they *don't* come back," replied Ms. Colman. "That happens. I think you would have gotten along all right, though."

"Yeah. I would have."

"I missed you last month."

"We missed you, too. But Mrs. Hoffman turned out to be okay. She taught us a lot about manners."

"So I hear."

I almost went to my seat. Then I remembered something. "Ms. Colman? Are we going to have our pizza party soon?"

Ms. Colman smiled. "I was just going to make an announcement about that," she said.

About the Author

ANN M. MARTIN lives in New York City and loves animals, especially cats. She has two cats of her own, Mouse and Rosie.

Other books by Ann M. Martin that you might enjoy are *Stage Fright*; *Me and Katie (the Pest)*; and the books in *The Baby-sitters Club* series.

Ann likes ice cream and *I Love Lucy*. And she has her own little sister, whose name is Jane.

Little Sister

Don't miss #22

KAREN'S LITTLE WITCH

Melody and Hannie and I ran across the street. Then we ran to this big bush in front of Morbidda Destiny's house. We scrunched down behind it.

"Does anyone see Druscilla?" I asked.

"Nope," said Hannie and Melody.

We hid for the longest time. We watched and watched. Finally . . .

"Someone's coming out the front door!" I hissed.

Melody and Hannie and I leaned over as far as we could.

"It's Druscilla! It's the little witch!" said Hannie.

LITTLE APPLE®

BABYSITTERS
Little Sister®
by Ann M. Martin, author of *The Baby-sitters Club*®

☐ MQ44300-3	#1	Karen's Witch	$2.75
☐ MQ44259-7	#2	Karen's Roller Skates	$2.75
☐ MQ44299-7	#3	Karen's Worst Day	$2.75
☐ MQ44264-3	#4	Karen's Kittycat Club	$2.75
☐ MQ44258-9	#5	Karen's School Picture	$2.75
☐ MQ43651-1	#10	Karen's Grandmothers	$2.75
☐ MQ43650-3	#11	Karen's Prize	$2.75
☐ MQ43649-X	#12	Karen's Ghost	$2.75
☐ MQ43648-1	#13	Karen's Surprise	$2.75
☐ MQ43646-5	#14	Karen's New Year	$2.75
☐ MQ43645-7	#15	Karen's in Love	$2.75
☐ MQ43644-9	#16	Karen's Goldfish	$2.75
☐ MQ43643-0	#17	Karen's Brothers	$2.75
☐ MQ43642-2	#18	Karen's Home-Run	$2.75
☐ MQ43641-4	#19	Karen's Good-Bye	$2.95
☐ MQ44823-4	#20	Karen's Carnival	$2.75
☐ MQ44824-2	#21	Karen's New Teacher	$2.95
☐ MQ44833-1	#22	Karen's Little Witch	$2.95
☐ MQ44832-3	#23	Karen's Doll	$2.95
☐ MQ44859-5	#24	Karen's School Trip	$2.75
☐ MQ44831-5	#25	Karen's Pen Pal	$2.75
☐ MQ44830-7	#26	Karen's Ducklings	$2.75
☐ MQ44829-3	#27	Karen's Big Joke	$2.75
☐ MQ44828-5	#28	Karen's Tea Party	$2.75
☐ MQ44825-0	#29	Karen's Cartwheel	$2.75
☐ MQ45645-8	#30	Karen's Kittens	$2.75
☐ MQ45646-6	#31	Karen's Bully	$2.95
☐ MQ45647-4	#32	Karen's Pumpkin Patch	$2.95
☐ MQ45648-2	#33	Karen's Secret	$2.95
☐ MQ45650-4	#34	Karen's Snow Day	$2.95
☐ MQ45652-0	#35	Karen's Doll Hosital	$2.95

Available wherever you buy books, or use this order form.

Kristy is Karen's older stepsister, and she and her friends are...

by Ann M. Martin, author of *Baby-sitters Little Sister*™

Available wherever you buy books, or use this order form.

Scholastic Inc., P.O. Box 7502, 2931 East McCarty Street, Jefferson City, MO 65102

Please send me the books I have checked above. I am enclosing $_____ (please add $2.00 to cover shipping and handling). Send check or money order — no cash or C.O.D.s please.

Name _____

Address_____

City_____ State/Zip _____

Please allow four to six weeks for delivery. Offer good in the U.S. only. Sorry, mail orders are not available to residents of Canada. Prices subject to change.